BOOK 3

Lyric Moments

6 Expressive Solos for Late Intermediate Pianists

In late August of 1993, my daughter Summer was born. One week later, William Gillock, a treasured friend, mentor, and composer, died. At the one-year anniversary of these two momentous events, my mind was filled with many melodies—some happy, some sad, and others wistful. Most importantly, all were expressions of the intense emotions I was feeling at the time. These melodies became the foundation for *Lyric Moments,* Books 1 and 2.

In the years since those books were published, I have heard from students and teachers around the world about how these pieces have affected them. A teacher who loved teaching "A Special Place in My Heart" (Book 1) asked for permission to put words to it so her father could sing it at her sister's wedding. A teacher in Japan cried after she played "Summer's Dream" (Book 1) for me, because she said it made her think of her daughter. I have heard teenagers play "Lament" (Book 2) with such beauty and sadness that I know they feel the depth of emotion, even at a young age. These experiences have shown me that, no matter who we are or where we live, we all have emotions that we can share through music.

It is my hope that in *Lyric Moments,* Book 3, teachers and students will find new pieces with which they can express their innermost feelings. I offer my heartfelt wishes for "lyric moments" in your life.

Catherine Rollin

CONTENTS

Alfred Music Publishing Co., Inc.
P.O. Box 10003
Van Nuys, CA 91410-0003
alfred.com

ISBN-10: 0-7390-6886-5
ISBN-13: 978-0-7390-6886-1
Cover art: *Sunset at Sea,* 1911
Childe Hassam (1859-1935), Oil on canvas, 34 x 34 in. (86.4 x 86.4 cm)
Rose Art Museum, Brandeis University, Waltham, Massachusetts

In memory of my treasured friend
Dr. Bonnie Lynn Sherr

Sweet Elegy

Catherine Rollin

For my teacher, friend, and mentor
Dr. David Daniels

Lyric Nocturne

Catherine Rollin

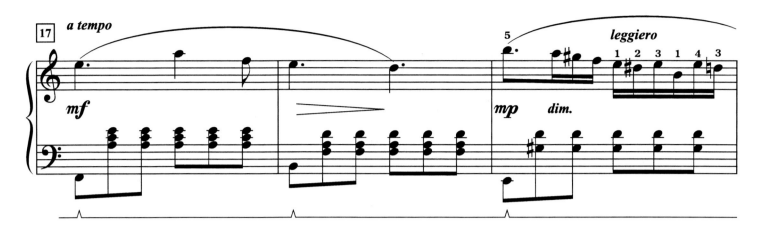

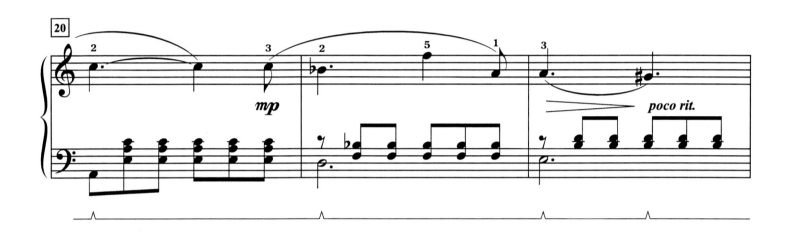

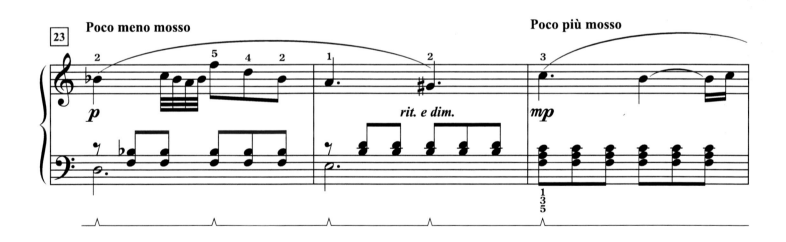

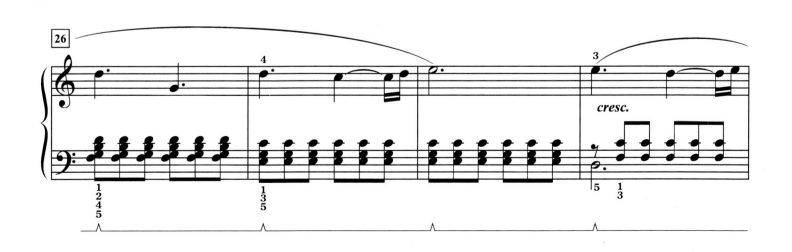

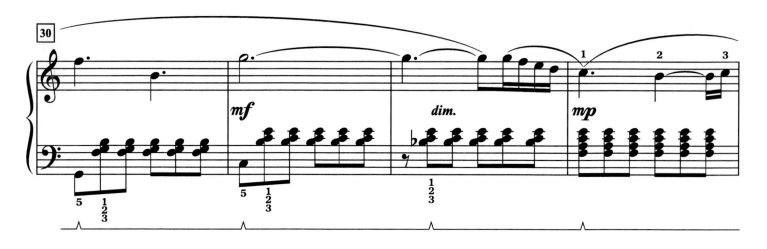

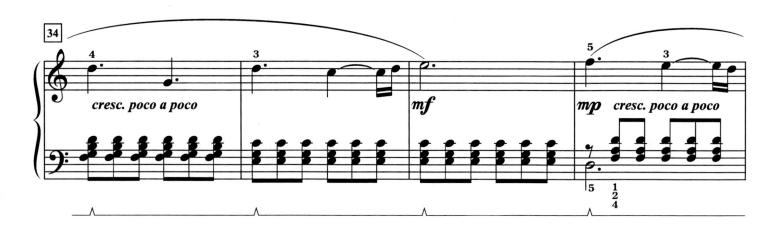

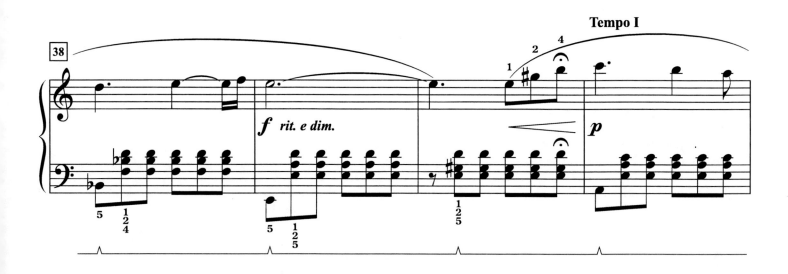

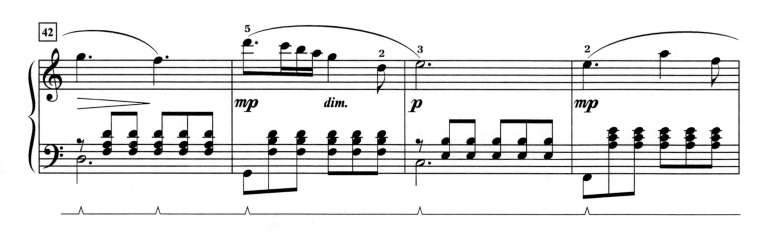

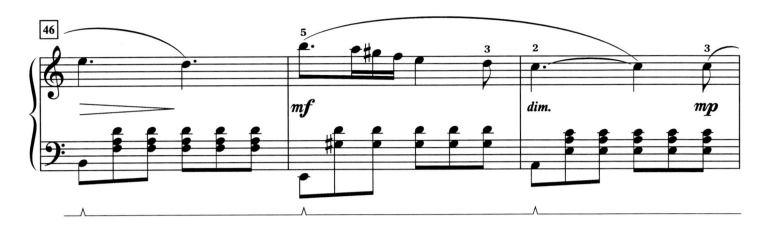

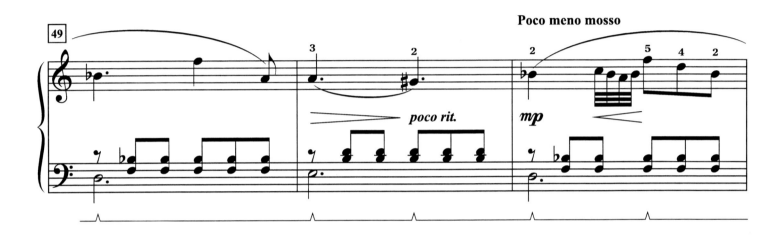

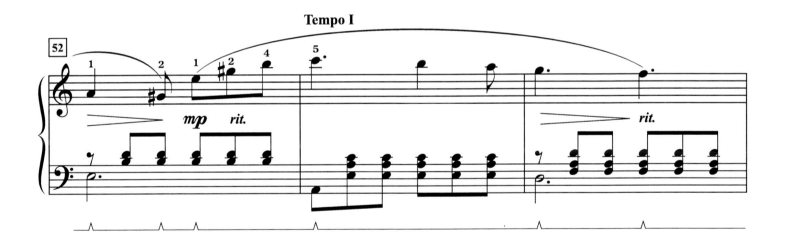

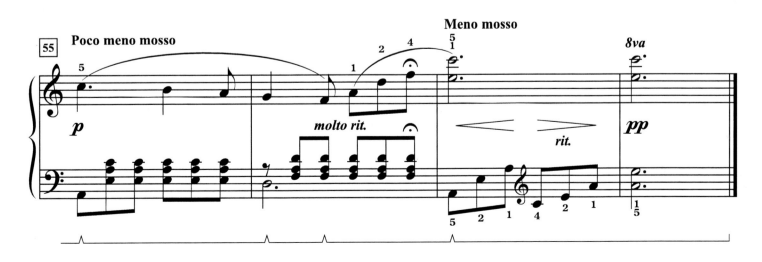

For Stephen Tu Grier

Tenderly

Catherine Rollin

Flowing moderately and gracefully

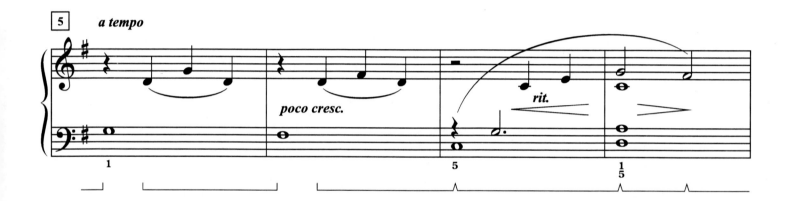

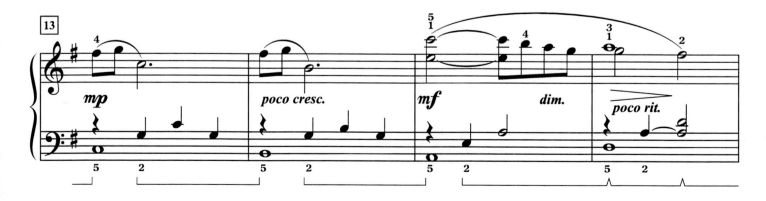

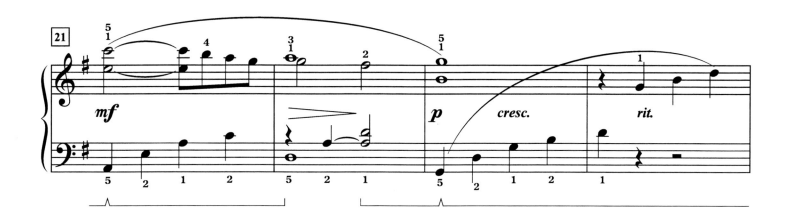

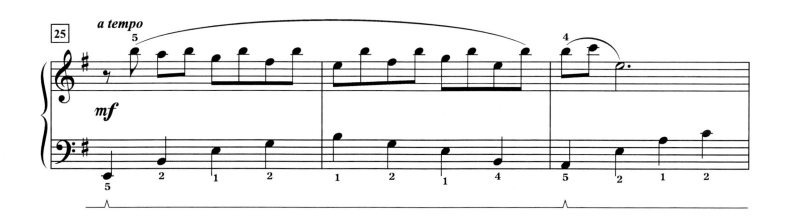

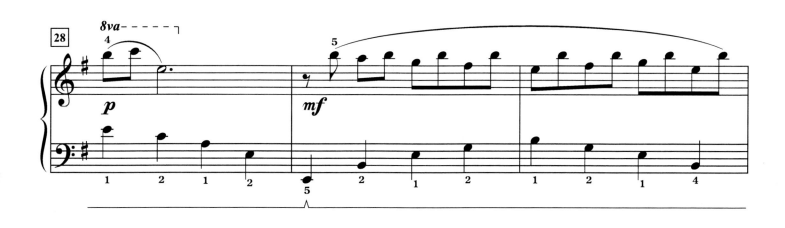

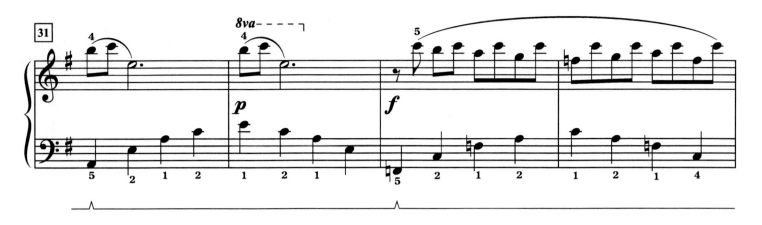

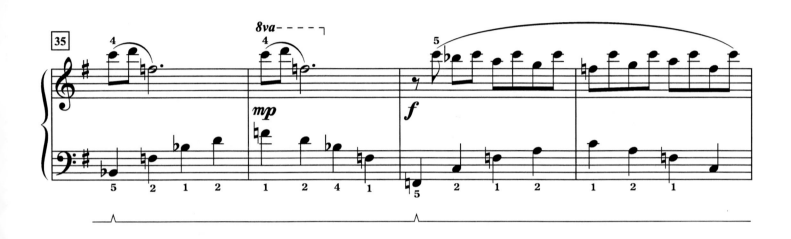

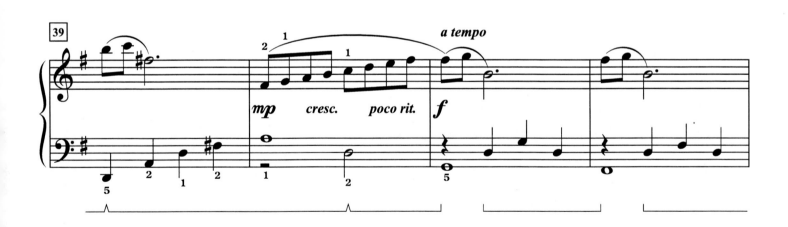

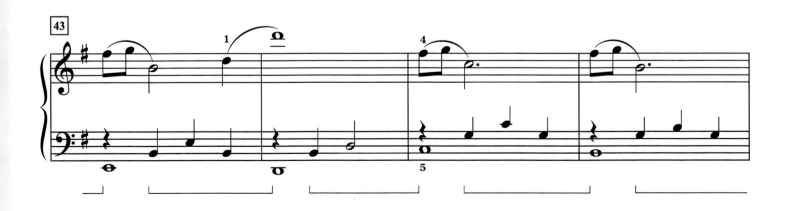

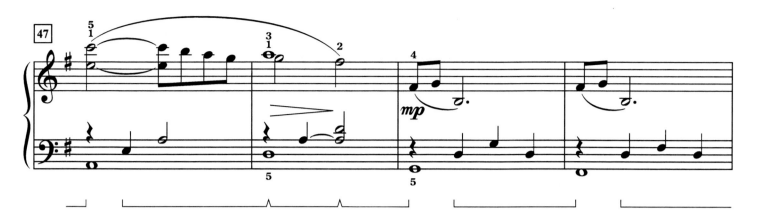

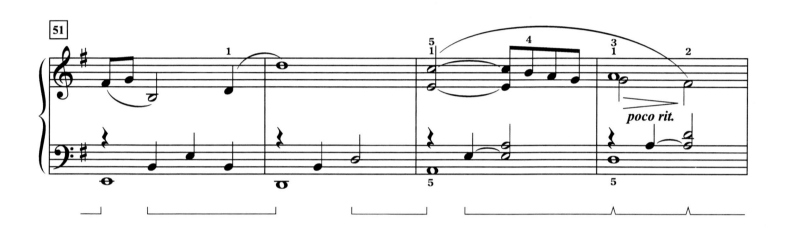

For Irwin

Pure Heart

Catherine Rollin

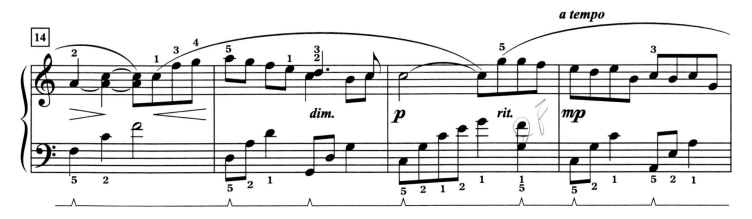

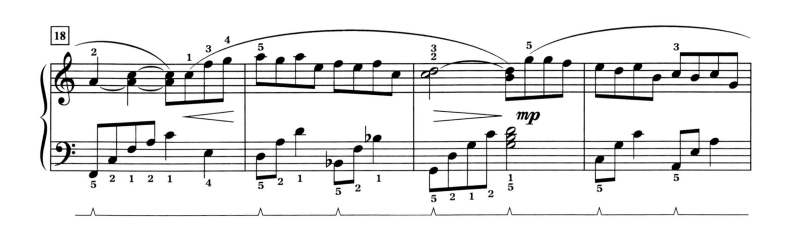

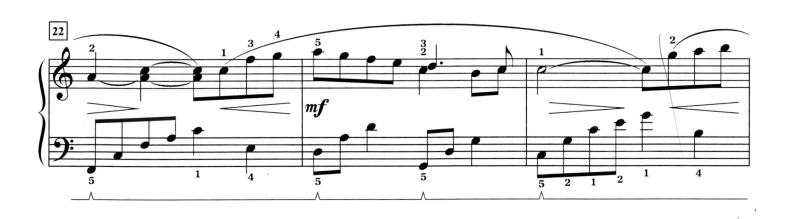

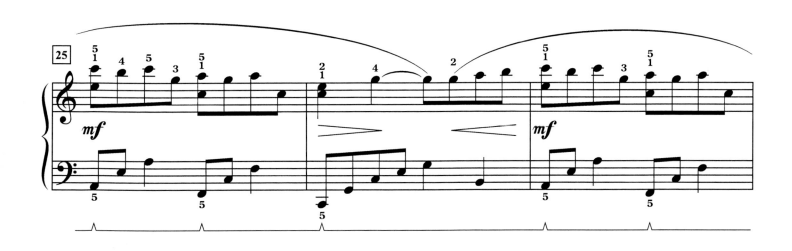

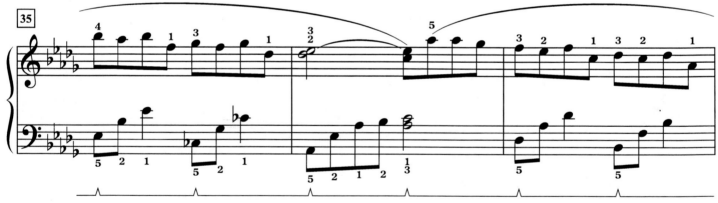

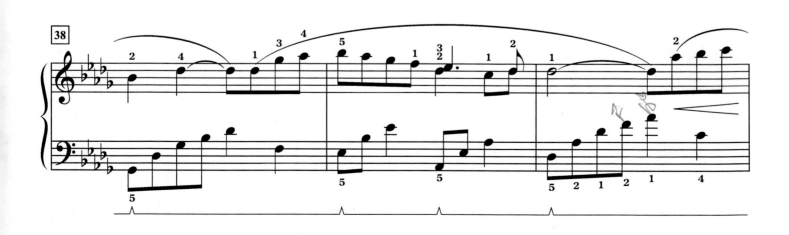

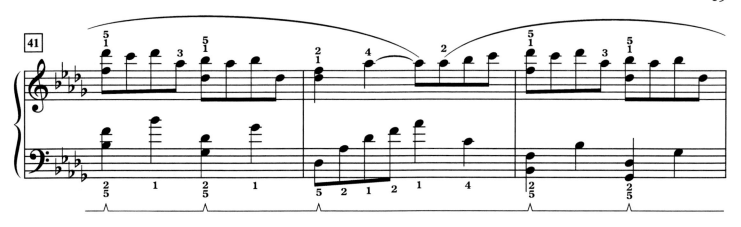

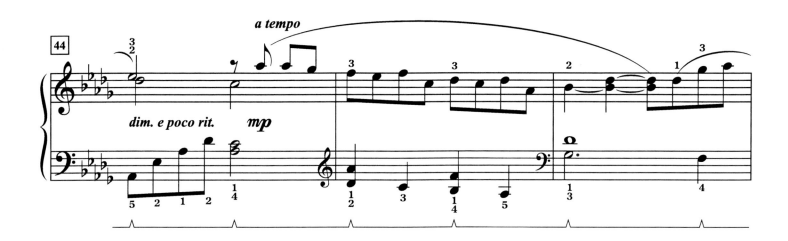

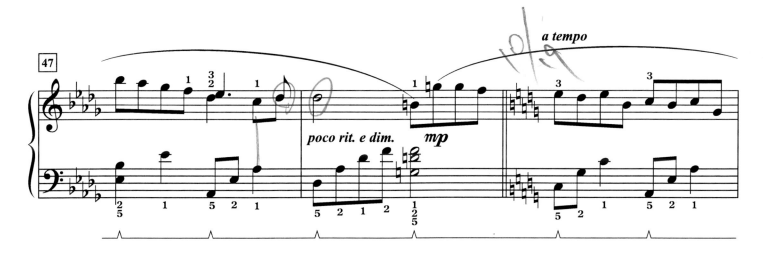

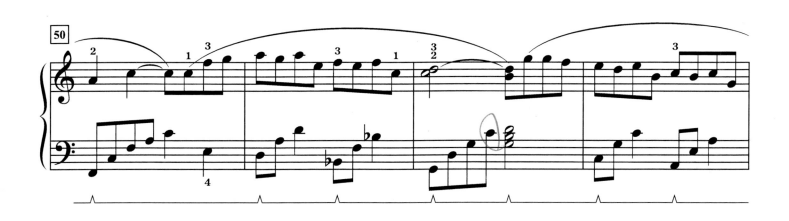

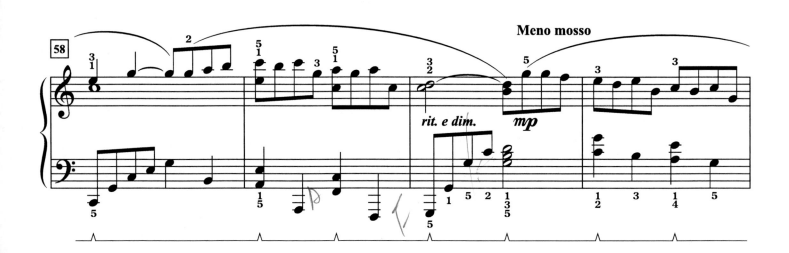

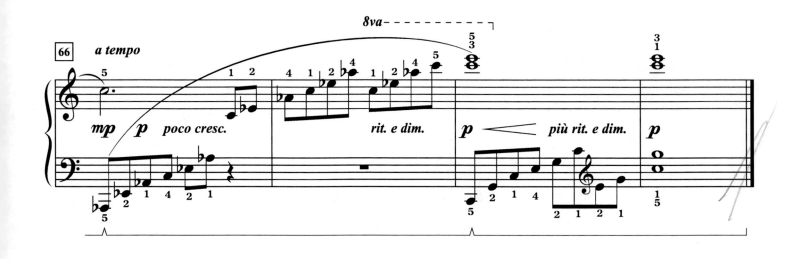

for Summer

Summer Splendor

Catherine Rollin

* The LH should be played very lightly to create a harmonic blend over which the RH can sing luminously.

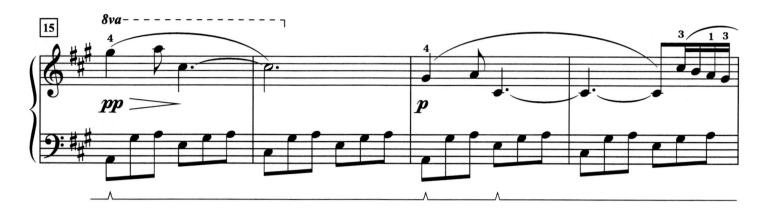

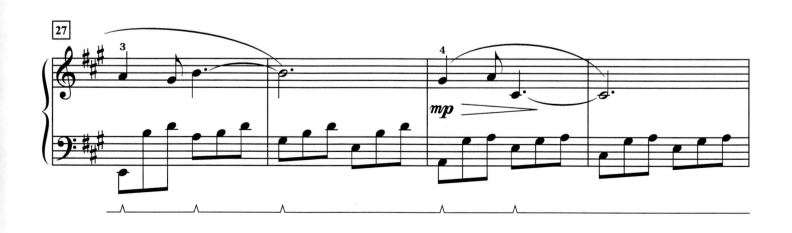

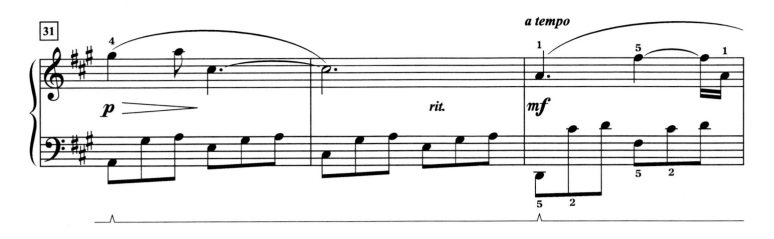

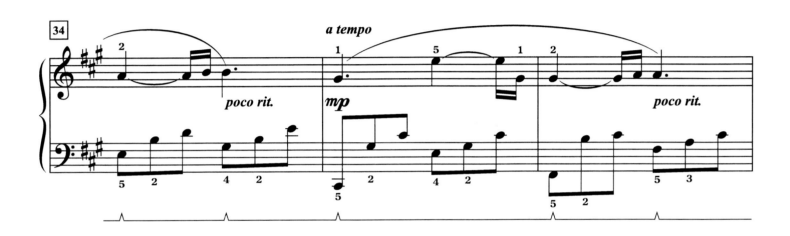

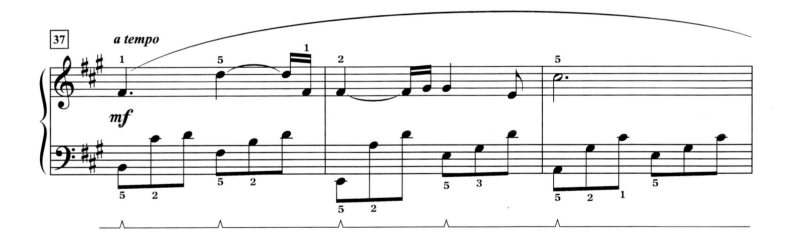

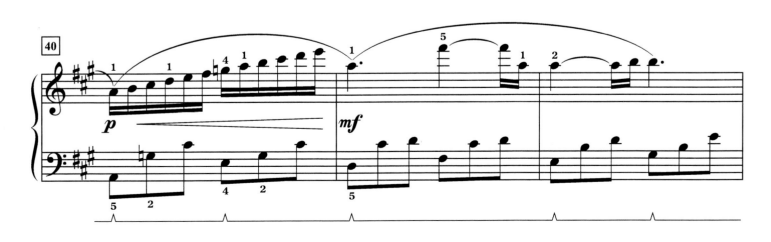

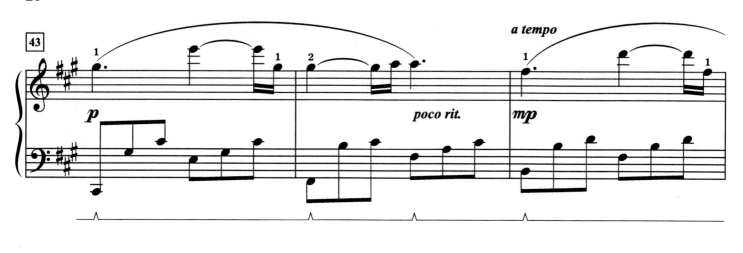

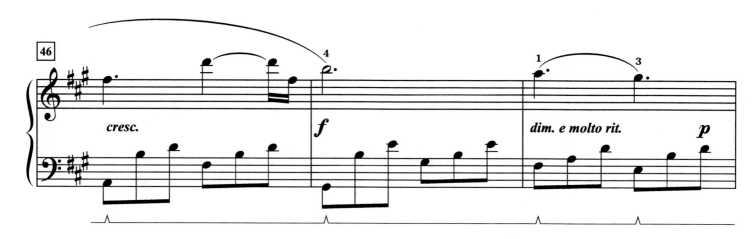

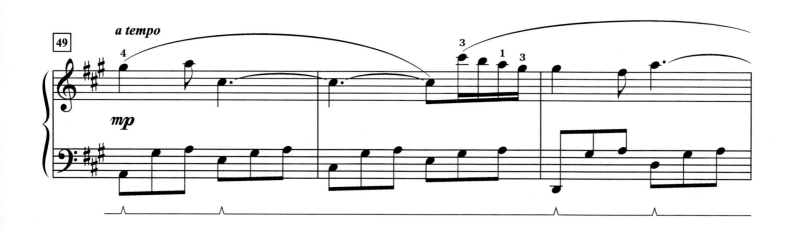

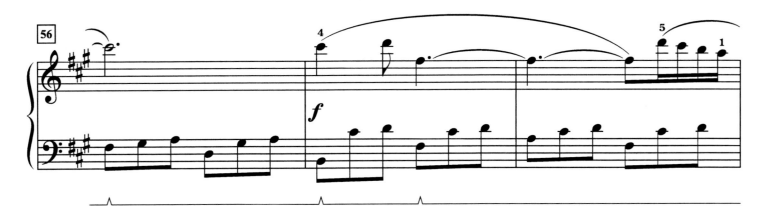

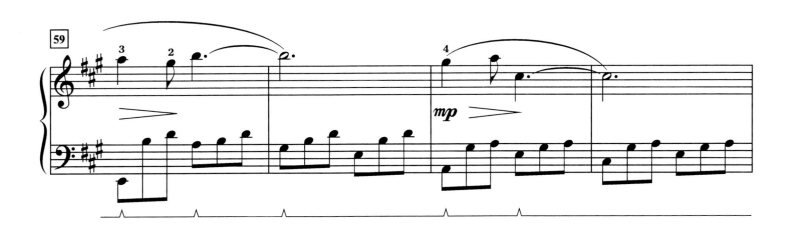

In memory of my friend Ann Ruth Kretzmer
who taught piano with love and dedication

Remembrance

Catherine Rollin

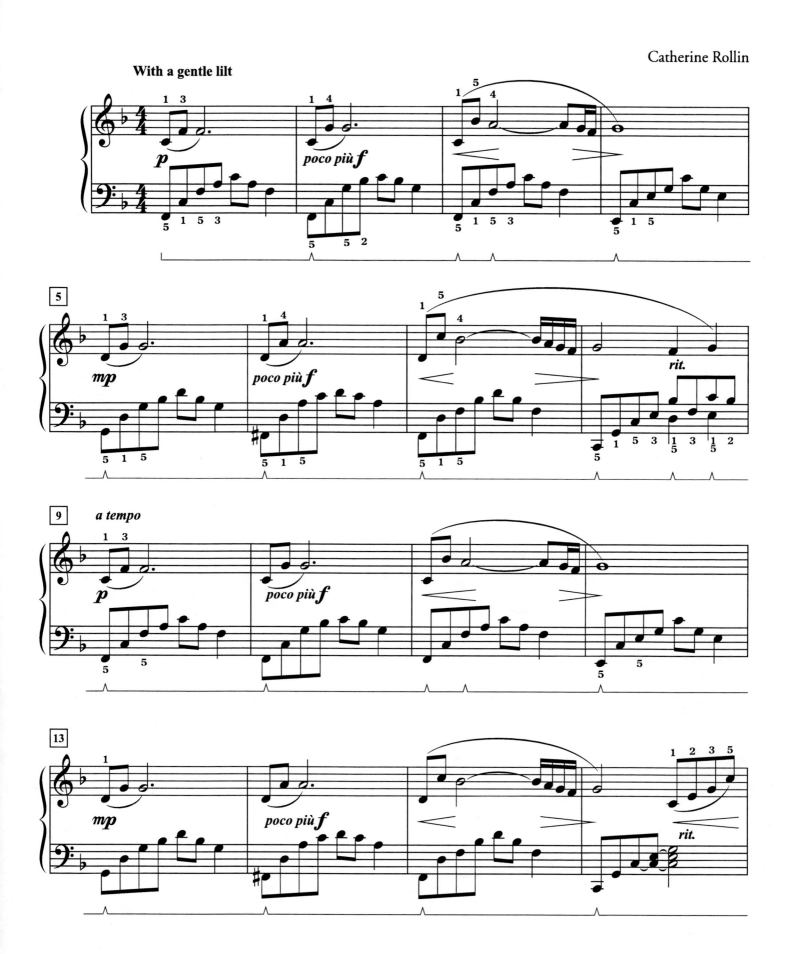

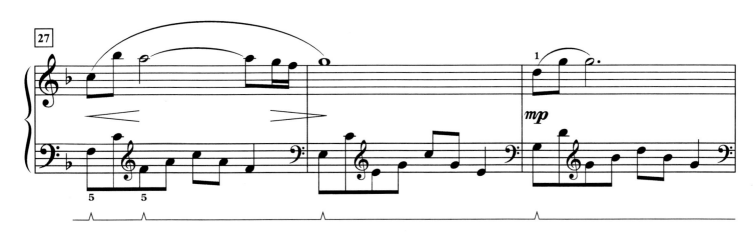

* In measures 17–18 and 21–22, the RH will be sustained by the pedal on beats 2 and 3.

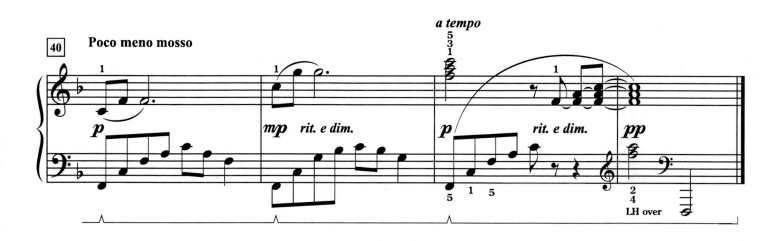

CATHERINE ROLLIN
Composer, teacher, pianist, clinician

PATHWAYS TO ARTISTRY

Repertoire
Book 1 (21368)
Book 2 (21369)
Book 3 (21370)

Technique
Book 1 (16597)
Book 2 (16598)
Book 3 (16599)

Masterworks
Book 1 (32148)
Book 2 (32149)
Book 3 (34014)

SOLO COLLECTIONS

American Medleys & Variations
(20777)—Intermediate

The Bean Bag Zoo Collector's Series
Book A (25401)—Early Elementary to
              Late Elementary
Book 1 (18777)—Elementary
Book 2 (18778)—Late Elementary

The Best of Catherine Rollin
Book 1 (18099)—Early Intermediate to
              Intermediate
Book 2 (18100)—Intermediate to
              Late Intermediate

Catherine Rollin's Favorite Solos
Book 1 (25391)—Early Elementary to
              Late Elementary
Book 2 (25392)—Early Intermediate to
              Intermediate
Book 3 (25393)—Intermediate to
              Late Intermediate

Christmas Impressions
Book 1 (6566)—Early Intermediate to
              Intermediate
Book 2 (6682)—Intermediate

Christmas Medleys and Variations
(21342)—Intermediate

Christmas Pleasures
(11744)—Intermediate

Circus Suite
(3228)—Late Elementary

Dances for Christmas
Book 1 (31459)—Early Intermediate to
              Intermediate
Book 2 (31460)—Intermediate

Dancing on the Keys
Book 1 (28287)—Early Intermediate
Book 2 (28288)—Intermediate

The Great Frontier!
(18182)—Late Elementary to
        Early Intermediate

Jazz-a-Little, Jazz-a-Lot
Book 1 (6659)—Late Elementary
Book 2 (6660)—Early Intermediate
Book 3 (31998)—Intermediate to
              Late Intermediate

Jazz Gems
(881294)—Early Intermediate

Jazz Menagerie
Book 1 (14743)—Early Intermediate
Book 2 (14744)—Early Intermediate

Lyric Moments
Book 1 (14663)—Intermediate
Book 2 (14664)—Intermediate
Book 3 (34662)—Late Intermediate
CD recording (Books 1 & 2) (14052)

The New Virtuoso
(3610)—Intermediate

Out of This World!
(11708)—Intermediate

Preludes for Piano
Book 1 (3609)—Intermediate
Book 2 (6039)—Intermediate

Romantic Gems
(881295)—Intermediate

Sounds of Spain
Book 1 (17601)—Early Intermediate to
              Intermediate
Book 2 (17602)—Intermediate
Book 3 (30108)—Late Intermediate

Spotlight on Baroque Style
(6037)—Early Intermediate to
        Intermediate

Spotlight on Christmas
(18761)—Intermediate

Spotlight on Classical Style
(6038)—Intermediate

Spotlight on Impressionist Style
(14707)—Intermediate

Spotlight on Jazz Style
(6509)—Early Intermediate to
        Intermediate

Spotlight on Ragtime Style
(6017)—Intermediate

Spotlight on Romantic Style
(6005)—Intermediate

Summer Vacation
(16609)—Early Intermediate

SOLO SHEETS

Early Elementary

Bean Bag Zoo
  Creepy Crocodile (18172)
  Octopuses All Have 8 (18981)

Elementary

Chocolate Chip Cookies (19752)

Bean Bag Zoo
  Bean Bag Dog (18534)
  King Lion (18173)
  Kitty Kat Meow (18174)
  My Bean Bear (18175)
  My Ducks Love to Quack (18176)
  A Tall Giraffe (18177)

Late Elementary

Cool Ghoul (5451)
Fiesta de Seville (32833)
Halloween Whodunit? (14334)
Handsprings (21401)
Hoe Down (17069)
Hot Chili Peppers (29133)
The Knight's Tale (24531)
Lefty's Cool Strut (22465)
Lizards (22411)
Mr. Jazz Man (30583)
Rock It (17595)
Rockin' the Blues (34301)
Sneaky Skeleton (5452)
Spooky Footsteps (14230)
Sunlight Waltz (18134)
The Swan (19774)
Witches' Brew (3666)
With a Yo-Ho-Ho! (24187)

Bean Bag Zoo
  Bean Bag Butterfly (18178)
  The Kangaroo That Almost Flew!
   (18179)
  Rockadoodle Cockadoodle!
   (18180)
  The Shark! (18181)

Early Intermediate

Butterscotch Rag (22400)
Dreams (25924)
El Conquistador (3647)
Howlin' Halloween (14232)
Jazz Hound (5431)
Jazzy Old Saint Nicholas (5432)
Legends of the Canyon (20747)
Sarabande d'Amour (27598)
Summer Ballad (14279)
Tendresse (19684)
Winter Waltz (14205)
Wish Upon a Star (22442)

Intermediate

Ballad for Our Time (19763)
Deck the Halls (18760)
Dreams of the Heart (18872)
Jazz Cat (3639)
Jazzin' in C (3611)
Moonlight Nocturne (28192)
Morning Reverie (21318)
Night Dance (88398)
Nights in Spain (3644)
Peanut Butter Rag (5309)
Rock Ballad (5417)
Stars and Wind (14220)
Summer's Nocturne (5466)
Sunflowers and Wheat Fields (22480)

Late Intermediate

Great American Boogie Woogie (3643)
Song of Hope (21339)
Twilight Dreams (21361)

RECITAL SUITES

The Grand Canyon
(34423)—Intermediate

Mississippi Moods
(21397)—Intermediate

Suite Georgia
(31913)—Late Intermediate

DUET COLLECTIONS

Dances for Two
Book 1 (19678)—Early Intermediate to
              Intermediate
Book 2 (19679)—Intermediate

The Nutcracker Suite for Two
(16919)—Intermediate to Late
        Intermediate

We Wish You a Jazzy Christmas
(16882)—Early Intermediate

DUET SHEETS

Carol of the Bells (18976)—Intermediate
Celebration Overture
  (18079)—Intermediate
Fiesta for Two (29195)—Intermediate
The Grand Finale
  (19744)—Late Intermediate
Valse Sentimentale à Deux
  (18073)—Intermediate
Winter Story (5474)—Early Intermediate

DUOS
(2 PIANOS, 4 HANDS)

Concerto in C Major
(5448)—Intermediate

Concerto Romantique
(18075)—Intermediate

Christmas for Sharing
(23271)—Intermediate

ISBN-10: 0-7390-6886-5
ISBN-13: 978-0-7390-6886-1

9 780739 068861

Alfred
alfred.com

34662 $6.99 in USA

0 38081 38745 1
ISBN 0-7390-6886-5